At the Market

Sally Cowan

Australia • Brazil • Japan • Korea • Mexico • Singapore • Spain • United Kingdom • United States

At the Market

Text: Sally Cowan
Editor: Rochelle Ransom
Design: Ami-Louise Sharpe
Series design: James Lowe
Photo researcher: Libby Henry
Production controller: Lisa Porter

Acknowledgements
The author and publisher would like to acknowledge permission to reproduce material from the following sources:
Corbis: pp. 8–9; iStockphoto/Maceofoto: p. 3; iStockphoto/Maksim Shmeljov: p. 16; Photolibrary: pp. 1, 4, 5, 6, 7 (main), 7 (inset), 10, 11, 12, 13 (main), 13 (inset), 14, 15, cover, back cover.

Every effort has been made to trace and acknowledge copyright. However, if any infringement has occurred, the publishers tender their apologies and invite the copyright holders to contact them.

Fast Forward Independent Texts
Level 6

For product information and technology assistance,
in Australia call 1300 790 853;
in New Zealand call 0508 635 766

For permission to use material from this text or product,
please email **aust.permissions@cengage.com**

ISBN 978 0 17 018087 0
ISBN 978 0 17 017896 9 (set)

Cengage Learning Australia
Level 7, 80 Dorcas Street
South Melbourne, Victoria Australia 3205

Cengage Learning New Zealand
Unit 4B Rosedale Office Park
331 Rosedale Road, Albany, North Shore NZ 0632

For learning solutions, visit **cengage.com.au**

Printed in Australia by Ligare Pty Ltd
3 4 5 6 7 8 9 20 19 18 17 16

At the Market

Sally Cowan

Contents

CHAPTER 1

Big City Markets

People buy and sell things at markets.

The **stall holders** get to the markets when most people are still asleep.

They set up the **stalls** to sell food, such as fruit, meat and fish.

Lots of people come to shop at big city markets.

Stall holders call out what is **on special**.

This stall has a lot of oranges. The oranges are on special.

People can buy clothes, shoes, bags and toys at markets, too.

People can get all the things they need at big city markets.

Night Markets

In summer,
people like to go to night markets.
They take time to look at the stalls
and walk around.

Some stalls sell hand-made clothes
and things for the home.

Other stalls sell cooked food to eat.

There is a lot to see and hear at night markets.

Farmers' Markets

At farmers' markets,
farmers sell food from their farms.

People like to buy the food because it is very **fresh**.

Some farmers have animals
on their farms.

Farmers sell food
that comes from the animals,
such as cheese and eggs.

Some stalls sell home-made cakes and jams.

People like to be outside
at farmers' markets.
They can have a good day out.

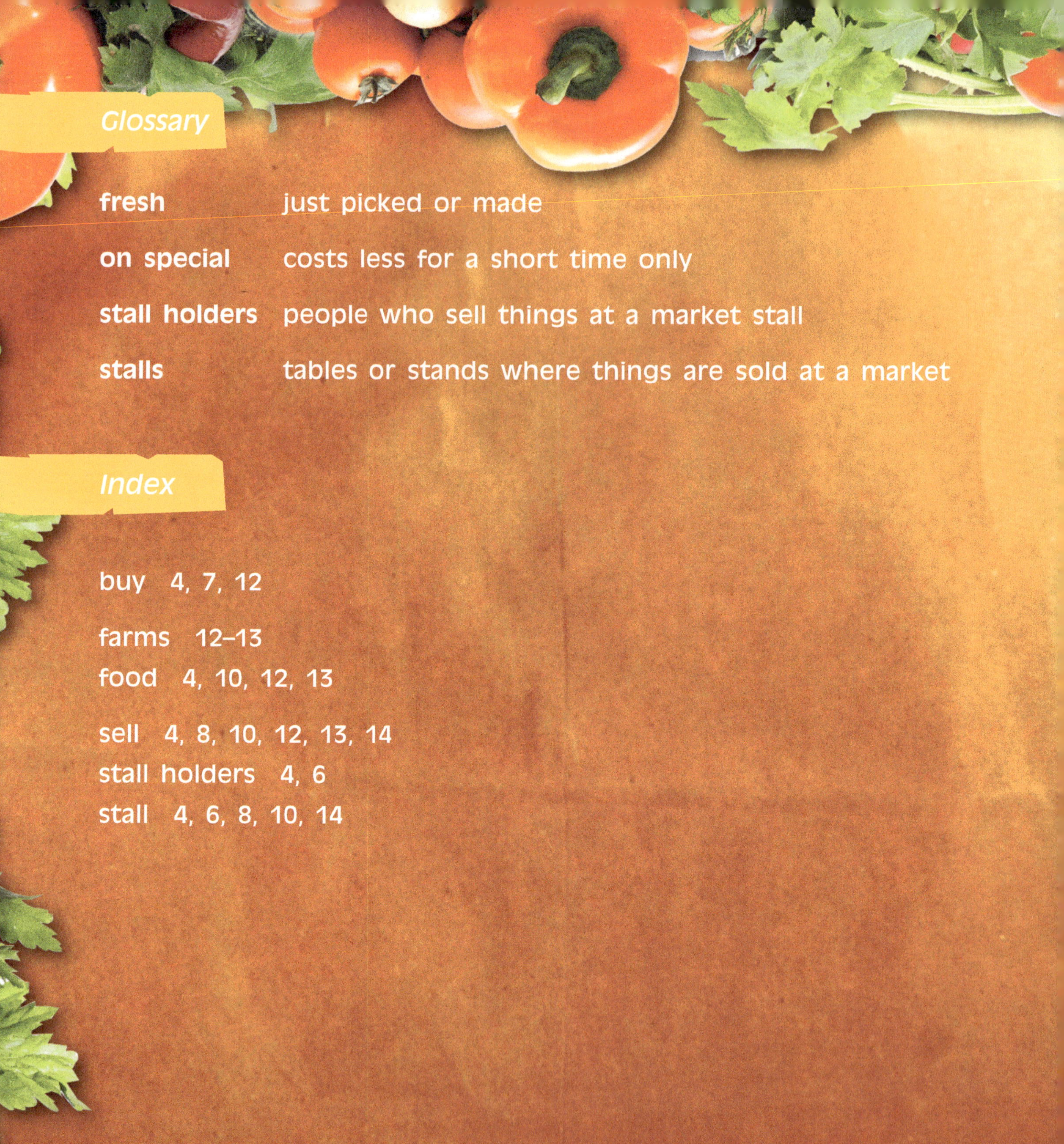

Glossary

fresh just picked or made

on special costs less for a short time only

stall holders people who sell things at a market stall

stalls tables or stands where things are sold at a market

Index